STAR WARS™

ULTIMATE STICKER COLLECTION

T0188533

How to use this book

Read the captions, then find the sticker that best fits the space. (Hint: check the sticker labels for clues!)

•

There are lots of fantastic extra stickers for creating your own scenes throughout the book.

DK | Penguin Random House

Written by Shari Last
Edited by Shari Last and Matt Jones
Designed by Mark Richards
Senior Designer Clive Savage
Senior Pre-Production Producer Jennifer Murray
Senior Producer Mary Slater
Managing Editor Sadie Smith
Managing Art Editor Vicky Short
Publisher Julie Ferris
Art Director Lisa Lanzarini
Publishing Director Simon Beecroft

For Lucasfilm

Assistant Editor Samantha Holland
Creative Director of Publishing Michael Siglain
Art Director Troy Alders
Story Group James Waugh, Pablo Hidalgo,
Matt Martin, and Leland Chee
Image Unit Steve Newman, Tim Mapp,
Gabrielle Levenson, Erik Sanchez, and Bryce Pinkos

First American Edition, 2018
Published in the United States by DK Publishing
1745 Broadway, 20th Floor, New York, NY 10019

For the curious

www.dk.com

THE JEDI

The Jedi are a group of brave warriors who want to protect the galaxy. They use a mysterious power called the Force to become wise and strong. This helps them defeat their enemies. Jedi come from all over the galaxy—they can be from any planet or any species.

OBI-WAN KENOBI

Obi-Wan Kenobi is brave and smart. He is often sent on important Jedi missions.

Luke Skywalker
Luke didn't realize he had such strong Force powers. Now he is one of the greatest Jedi of all time!

KIT FISTO

Kit Fisto is a green-skinned Jedi from the ocean planet Glee Anselm. He is a fierce fighter on the battlefield.

MACE WINDU

Mace Windu is known for being wise. Many other Jedi come to him for advice. He is also famous for his purple lightsaber blade.

QUI-GON JINN

Qui-Gon is a Jedi Master. This means he trains younger Jedi, who are known as Padawans. Qui-Gon is kind and strong-minded.

AAYLA SECURA

This smart Jedi is a Twi'lek from the planet Ryloth. Aayla is brave and very skilled with a lightsaber.

ANAKIN SKYWALKER

Anakin is one of the most powerful Jedi of all time. He is an expert pilot and incredibly strong with the Force.

PLO KOON

Plo Koon is calm and wise. He is from the planet Dorin and has to wear a breathing mask and goggles when he travels to different planets.

YODA

Wise Master Yoda is the leader of the Jedi. He is very small, but very powerful. Yoda uses the Force to feel what is going on across the galaxy.

THE SITH

The Sith are the ancient enemies of the Jedi. They also use the Force, but they study the dark side of the Force, which makes them very powerful and dangerous. The Sith are secretive and cunning. They try to carry out their evil plans without anyone noticing.

EMPEROR PALPATINE

Cloaked and mysterious, Emperor Palpatine is a dangerous Sith Lord. He wants to rule over the whole galaxy.

Darth Vader

Darth Vader is Emperor Palpatine's second-in-command. He wears body armor and a breathing mask to keep him alive. Vader is known to have a very bad temper. Scary!

COUNT DOOKU

Count Dooku was once a Jedi, but he turned to the dark side of the Force. Now, he is a Sith named Darth Tyranus.

DARTH MAUL

This highly-trained Sith has scary tattoos all over his face and body. Maul carries a terrifying double-bladed lightsaber, and is not afraid to use it!

DEATH STAR

This deadly battle station is as big as a moon and much more dangerous! Its superlaser can destroy an entire planet.

EXECUTOR

Darth Vader's gigantic starship is called *Executor*. Vader commands the stormtrooper army from aboard this ship.

SITH INFILTRATOR

Darth Maul has his own stealthy starship called the *Scimitar*. It is armed with six deadly laser cannons and can travel through space undetected.

HEROES

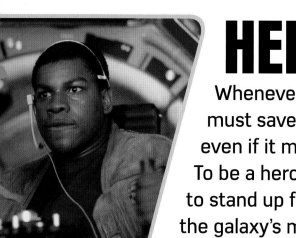

Whenever the galaxy is under threat, heroes must save the day. They charge to the rescue, even if it means putting themselves in danger. To be a hero you must be brave, kind, and ready to stand up for what's right. Let's meet some of the galaxy's most famous heroes.

FINN

Finn used to be a stormtrooper called FN-2187. After meeting Poe Dameron and Rey, he switches sides and becomes a hero.

PADMÉ AMIDALA

Padmé is a leader from the planet Naboo. She works hard to make the galaxy safe for everyone.

REY

Rey used to live on a quiet planet called Jakku. She never thought she would end up training to become a Jedi!

ADMIRAL HOLDO

Admiral Holdo will do anything to protect the galaxy from deadly threats, even if it places her in danger.

JYN ERSO

Jyn never planned on being a hero. But when the galaxy is under threat, she leads a dangerous mission to find the plans for the Death Star.

ADMIRAL ACKBAR
This war hero from the planet Mon Cala is brilliant at leading troops and thinking up battle plans.

HAN SOLO AND CHEWBACCA
Han and his Wookiee friend Chewbacca are the pilots of the *Millennium Falcon*. They always look out for each other.

POE DAMERON
Poe is one of the fastest X-wing pilots in the galaxy! He loves speeding into battle.

ROSE TICO
Rose is an engineer. She shows her courage when she joins Finn on a secret undercover mission.

General Organa
Leia Organa is a brave, strong leader. She is not afraid to stand up for what is right.

VILLAINS

Watch out! Villains are always plotting their next evil scheme. Some want to become all powerful and rule the galaxy. Others want to wipe out every single Jedi. Some even build superweapons so they can destroy entire planets. Here are some of the worst villains the galaxy has ever seen.

GENERAL GRIEVOUS

Part living being, part machine, General Grievous is a scary cyborg warrior who leads an army of droids against the Jedi.

Kylo Ren

Kylo Ren is dangerous. He is full of fear, doubt, and rage. Most of all, he wants to rule the galaxy.

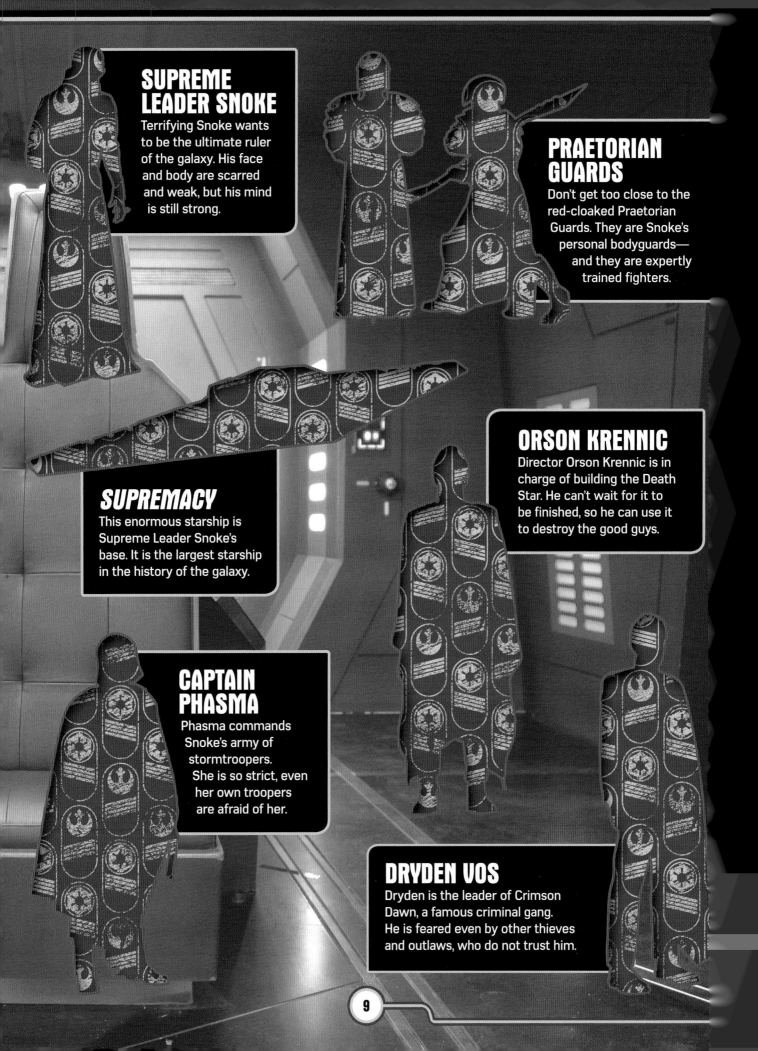

SUPREME LEADER SNOKE
Terrifying Snoke wants to be the ultimate ruler of the galaxy. His face and body are scarred and weak, but his mind is still strong.

PRAETORIAN GUARDS
Don't get too close to the red-cloaked Praetorian Guards. They are Snoke's personal bodyguards— and they are expertly trained fighters.

ORSON KRENNIC
Director Orson Krennic is in charge of building the Death Star. He can't wait for it to be finished, so he can use it to destroy the good guys.

SUPREMACY
This enormous starship is Supreme Leader Snoke's base. It is the largest starship in the history of the galaxy.

CAPTAIN PHASMA
Phasma commands Snoke's army of stormtroopers. She is so strict, even her own troopers are afraid of her.

DRYDEN VOS
Dryden is the leader of Crimson Dawn, a famous criminal gang. He is feared even by other thieves and outlaws, who do not trust him.

TROOPERS

Armies of white-armored stormtroopers can be seen across the galaxy. They are the soldiers of the evil Empire and, later, the dangerous First Order. Stormtroopers have been trained since they were very young and are expert fighters. They help to keep each planet under control.

SNOWTROOPER

Snowtroopers wear armor with built-in heating controls. This keeps them warm on ice-covered planets.

SCOUT TROOPER

These specially trained troopers are sent to spy on their enemies. They fly super-fast speeder bikes.

FLAMETROOPER

Flametroopers wear fireproof armor and carry powerful flamethrower weapons. They scare their enemies away with huge flames.

SANDTROOPER

On desert planets, sandtroopers wear special armor and masks to stay cool and keep the scratchy sand out.

SPEEDER BIKE

Speeder bikes zoom incredibly fast above the ground. They can zip over rocks and between trees with ease.

Stormtrooper
Protected by their white armor, stormtroopers make sure everybody listens to the rules.

AT-AT
All terrain armored transports (AT-ATs) are huge walking machines. They scare enemies during battle. Each AT-AT has four laser cannons. Run!

AT-AT PILOT
AT-AT pilots undergo intense training to learn how to operate a towering AT-AT walking machine.

DROIDS

Do you like droids? They come in all shapes and sizes and are programmed to carry out many different jobs. Some droids are very loyal and even make friends with their owners. Over time, a droid might develop its own unique personality. They can be nervous, loyal, bossy, or even rude!

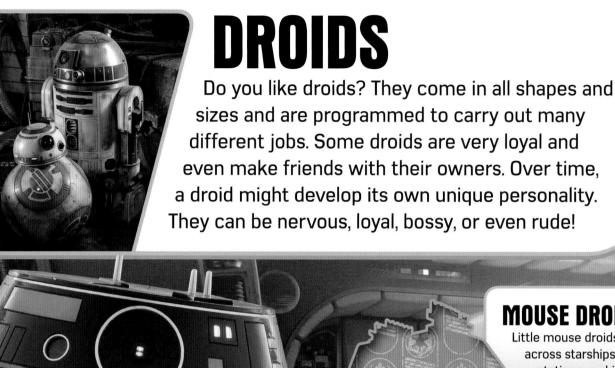

MOUSE DROID
Little mouse droids scuttle across starships and battle stations, making repairs or delivering messages.

C-3PO
This clever droid can speak over 7 million languages! C-3PO is very useful to his masters, although danger makes him nervous.

R2-D2
R2-D2 is an astromech droid. Astromechs helps pilots fly their starships. R2-D2 is quite cheeky, and he has lots of amazing gadgets.

BB-9E
BB-9E is a nasty astromech droid. He is very good at catching spies.

K-2SO
K-2SO used to be an Imperial security droid, but he joins the good guys. His mechanical body is extremely strong.

L3-37
L3 built herself out of old parts. She wants everyone to treat droids kindly and gets very cross if they do not.

PZ-4CO
This tall blue droid assists General Leia Organa in the control room. She helps Leia communicate with her officers.

BB-8
This little round astromech droid belongs to X-wing pilot Poe Dameron.

BATTLE DROIDS

During the Clone Wars, the Jedi fought many battles against a terrifying droid army. Droid armies are dangerous because they can be built quickly and have many powerful weapons. However, some battle droids cannot think for themselves, so they are slow to react during battle.

BUZZ DROID
Buzz droids look cute, but they are actually very dangerous! They attach onto enemy starships and destroy them using sharp saws and drills.

VULTURE DROID
Vulture droids swoop through the air at fast speeds. When they land, their wings can turn into walking legs.

TANK DROID
These big, tough droids can roll across land or through water. Their powerful treads crush everything in their path.

BATTLE DROID
These spindly droids march into battle, ready to fire their blasters. They fight well but are still no match for a Jedi.

DWARF SPIDER DROID
Small spider droids can travel across any terrain thanks to their four legs. They are also agile enough to crawl through narrow spaces.

HAILFIRE DROID
Hailfire droids are like big, rolling tanks. They can destroy enemy vehicles with a single blast from their missile launchers.

DROIDEKA
Deadly droidekas curl into balls and roll onto the battlefield. Their blaster cannons and defense shields make them very hard to defeat.

Super Battle Droid
These big droids are smarter than regular battle droids. They also have blasters built into their arms.

VEHICLES

Zooooom! Most vehicles are designed and built for different purposes. It is important to choose the perfect vehicle for your mission. Are you flying in ice-cold conditions, taking part in a race, or having a big party? Here are lots of different vehicles. Which one would you choose?

SAIL BARGE
Crime lord Jabba the Hutt loves inviting his criminal friends for parties aboard his sail barge, the *Khetanna*. It has large windows and a drinks bar.

LANDSPEEDER
Luke Skywalker pilots a trusty, dusty landspeeder on his homeworld Tatooine. It travels fast over the desert sand.

Podracer
Be careful—podracing is very a dangerous sport! Podracers can reach incredibly fast speeds.

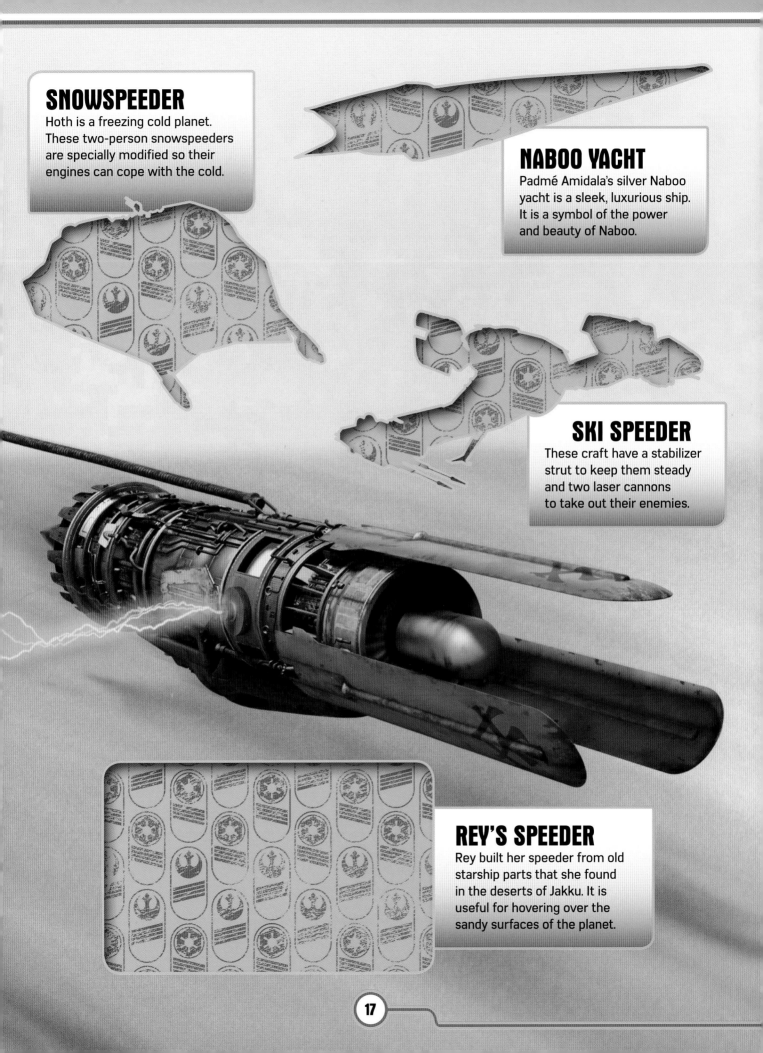

SNOWSPEEDER

Hoth is a freezing cold planet. These two-person snowspeeders are specially modified so their engines can cope with the cold.

NABOO YACHT

Padmé Amidala's silver Naboo yacht is a sleek, luxurious ship. It is a symbol of the power and beauty of Naboo.

SKI SPEEDER

These craft have a stabilizer strut to keep them steady and two laser cannons to take out their enemies.

REY'S SPEEDER

Rey built her speeder from old starship parts that she found in the deserts of Jakku. It is useful for hovering over the sandy surfaces of the planet.

STARSHIPS

From space battles to secret Jedi missions, starships are built for many different purposes. Some have lots of weapons, but can't travel at lightspeed. Others are light and fast, but don't have strong defense shields. Here are some of the galaxy's most well-known vehicles.

T-70 X-wing
T-70 X-wing fighters are more powerful and faster than the older T-65 X-wing starfighters.

JEDI INTERCEPTOR
Obi-Wan Kenobi's Jedi starfighter is a very light vehicle, which means it can fly extremely fast.

RESISTANCE BOMBER
These big bombers are not super speedy, but they can hold lots of bombs. When the bomber is in place, it drops hundreds of these bombs onto the target. Boom!

TIE FIGHTER
TIE fighters are small and speedy starfighters. Their engines emit a loud roar as they zoom off!

A-WING
This starfighter is perfect for quick strikes against the enemy. It is able to travel at lightspeed, so it can join a battle without warning and then quickly disappear.

U-WING
This large starship transports troops into battle. The U-wing's wings can swing backward to increase its wingspan and the range of its deflector shields.

SLAVE I
Slave I belongs to the famous bounty hunter Jango Fett, and later his son Boba. It has many laser cannons and missile launchers.

MILLENNIUM FALCON
Is this the fastest starship in the galaxy? Pilots Han Solo and Chewbacca certainly think so. The *Millennium Falcon* has a hyperdrive, which means the ship can travel at lightspeed.

Use the
extra stickers
to create your
own scene.

21

PLACES

Sandy, snowy, swampy, or stormy—there are millions of planets in the galaxy. Each one is unique, and many of them are home to different people and creatures. Where would you like to go? An underwater city? A tree-top village? A lonely mountain? Or a muddy swamp? Let's explore!

CORUSCANT

Coruscant is home to the galactic government. Huge skyscrapers are everywhere, and the busy sky highways are always full of speeders.

ENDOR

This forest moon is home to the little Ewoks. They live in tree-top villages that can be reached by ladders and bridges.

Coruscant
The whole planet of Coruscant is covered by one enormous city.

AHCH-TO

Ahch-To is far, far away from... everything. The planet is dotted with many small islands. On one of the islands, you can find the first Jedi temple!

HOTH

For endless ice, head to Hoth. There was once a big battle on Hoth, where small snowspeeders defeated huge AT-AT walkers.

DAGOBAH

Dagobah is a dark, swampy planet, covered in trees and mud. It's not very exciting, but it is an excellent place for a Jedi in danger to hide.

TATOOINE

Nothing much happens on this hot, sandy planet. Most of the people who live here work on farms that collect water.

CANTONICA

This planet has a famous casino where rich traders come to have fun. There are lots of thieves, rogues, and outlaws here, too.

NABOO

Naboo is a beautiful world, with grassy mountains, blue lakes, and pretty cities. Some of the cities are underwater!

ALIENS

Alien allies or alien foes? There are millions of different species in the galaxy and not all of them are friendly. Some team up with the Sith or other villains; while others join the Jedi and want peace. Many choose not to get involved, because they care only about their planet or themselves!

NIEN NUNB

Nien Nunb is from the planet Sullust. He used to be a smuggler, but now he is a top pilot. He helps to destroy the second Death Star.

JABBA THE HUTT

Jabba is from the planet Nal Hutta, and lives in a palace on Tatooine. He is a wicked crime lord, who works with criminals and bounty hunters!

WICKET W. WARRICK

Ewoks, like Wicket, are fierce warriors and loyal friends. They live in tree-top houses on the forest moon of Endor.

UNKAR PLUTT

Unkar is a tall, fish-like Crolute. He runs the junkyard at Niima Outpost on the planet Jakku. He is mean, greedy, and shouts a lot.

JAR JAR BINKS

Jar Jar is a Gungan from an underwater city on the planet Naboo. He is the friendliest Gungan you will ever meet!

CARETAKER

The Caretakers are from the Lanai species. They live on the island of Ahch-To and look after the very old buildings there.

TAUN WE

Taun We is a female Kaminoan from the stormy sea world of Kamino. Her species is very smart. They create an army of clone troopers.

Maz Kanata
Maz is not a Jedi, but she can feel the Force to understand people. She helps the good guys out.

THERM SCISSORPUNCH

Therm Scissorpunch is a hard-shelled Nephran who likes to play cards. He isn't very skilled, but his grim appearance scares his fellow players.

CREATURES

Each planet is home to all sorts of wonderful creatures. From cute and cuddly to big and slobbery, some will make you smile, while others will make you want to run away! Some creatures are strong, so they are used to carry heavy cargo. What crazy critters will you discover?

HAPPABORE

This strange looking creature with a huge snout lives on desert planets. It has thick skin, which protects it from the heat.

TAUNTAUN

These big snow-lizards live on the frozen planet Hoth. Their thick skin and white fur help them keep warm.

Porg
Fluffy little porgs live on the planet Ahch-To. They are curious and friendly.

BANTHA

Banthas are huge, strong, hairy creatures with big, curved horns. They can be used for transporting people or cargo.

FATHIER

Fathiers are large, graceful animals that can run extremely fast. They are gentle creatures, but be careful, their hooves are hard and dangerous.

VARACTYL

This varactyl has a name: Boga! He is a big lizard-like creature who once helped Obi-Wan Kenobi chase the villain General Grievous.

VULPTEX

These glittering, crystal-covered creatures live in tunnels of the salt-crusted planet Crait.

DEWBACK

Dewbacks are large lizards that live on the desert planet Tatooine. Some sandtroopers ride on them across the sand.

MONSTERS

Terrifying monsters lurk in the dark corners, caves, swamps, and deep oceans of the galaxy. Some have sharp teeth or claws, while others have slimy tentacles. Some are smaller than a human, while others are bigger than a starship! Whatever you do, keep away from these guys!

WAMPA

Wampas live in the icy caves of the planet Hoth. Their white fur helps them hide in the thick snow.

RANCOR

Scary rancors have very thick skin that can even withstand blaster fire. Their mouths are big: big enough to fit a whole person!

ACKLAY

An acklay is part-lizard, part-crab. It has six sharp claws, which are strong enough to crush its enemies.

SARLACC

Sarlaccs are enormous monsters with many tentacles. They live in big holes in the ground and eat whoever is unlucky enough to fall in.

SPACE SLUG

Huge space slugs live inside asteroids. Their enormous, long bodies are so big, people sometimes think they are actually caves!

NEXU

Even a small nexu can be scary. These fierce beasts have four eyes, sharp teeth, and prickly spikes all over their backs.

OPEE SEA KILLER

These massive creatures live deep in the oceans of the planet Naboo. Watch out for their two rows of spiky teeth!

Rathtar

Rathtars will eat anything with their huge, gaping mouth. If you see one, run!

ROGUES

If you're looking for a bounty hunter, thief, codebreaker, or smuggler—then look no further. These rogues do dangerous or illegal jobs for whoever will pay them. Some rogues are rotten to the core, but sometimes a rogue wants to do the right thing, and can even become a hero!

JANGO FETT

Jango Fett is a ruthless bounty hunter. He wears Mandalorian armor, which has many concealed weapons, as well as a jetpack.

BOBA FETT

Boba Fett is Jango Fett's son—and a bounty hunter, too! He works for many villains, including Darth Vader and Jabba the Hutt.

SIDON ITHANO

This mysterious pirate always wears a striking red helmet. He is known by his nickname, the Crimson Corsair.

IG-88

This deadly droid is an expert at hunting down or capturing people. His robotic eye can see in all directions.

LANDO CALRISSIAN

Lando is a card player and a smuggler. He used to own the *Millennium Falcon*, but lost it in a game of cards.

Han Solo
Han is a street thief, but he really wants to be a pilot. He will do anything to fly across the galaxy!

DJ
This con-artist says he can crack any code and unlock any door. He is only loyal to the person who pays him the most money. Watch out!

BOSSK
Bossk is a lizard-like Trandoshan. He is one of group of bounty hunters who are sent by Darth Vader to capture Han Solo.

GREEDO
Greedo is a bounty hunter from the planet Rodia. He works for Jabba the Hutt, who has paid him to capture Han Solo.

Use the extra stickers to create your own scene.

STICKERS

ANAKIN SKYWALKER

AAYLA SECURA

Captain Phasma's helmet

PLO KOON

YODA

QUI-GON JINN

MACE WINDU

OBI-WAN KENOBI

KIT FISTO

R2-D2

STICKERS

COUNT DOOKU

DEATH STAR

EMPEROR PALPATINE

Falcon

Stormtrooper

EXECUTOR

SITH INFILTRATOR

DARTH MAUL

STICKERS

ROSE TICO

REY

Speedy TIE Fighter

X-wing pilot's helmet

FINN

ADMIRAL HOLDO

PADMÉ AMIDALA

ADMIRAL ACKBAR

JYN ERSO

HAN SOLO AND CHEWBACCA

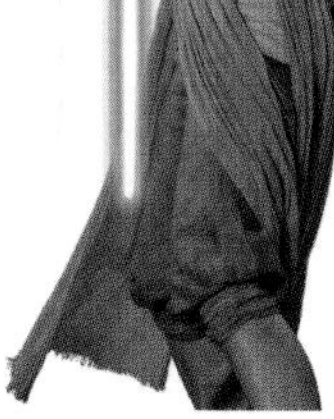

Rey in action

POE DAMERON

Bantha with Tusken Raider

© LFL

STICKERS

GENERAL GRIEVOUS

SUPREME LEADER SNOKE

CAPTAIN PHASMA

SUPREMACY

T-70 X-wing

Stormtrooper helmet

Darth Vader

Kylo Ren

PRAETORIAN GUARDS

Falcon from above

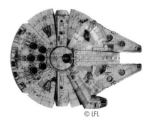

Ravenous rathtar

STICKERS

FLAMETROOPER

SCOUT TROOPER

SANDTROOPER

Luke Skywalker

Evil BB-9E

SNOWTROOPER

SPEEDER BIKE

Kylo Ren's lightsaber

AT-AT

General Grievous in battle

AT-AT PILOT

STICKERS

Powerful A-wing

General Organa

C-3PO

PZ-4CO

Yoda in action

K-2SO

Friendly BB-8

Poe's X-wing

Sebulba

Jedi Master Obi-Wan Kenobi

MOUSE DROID

R2-D2

STICKERS

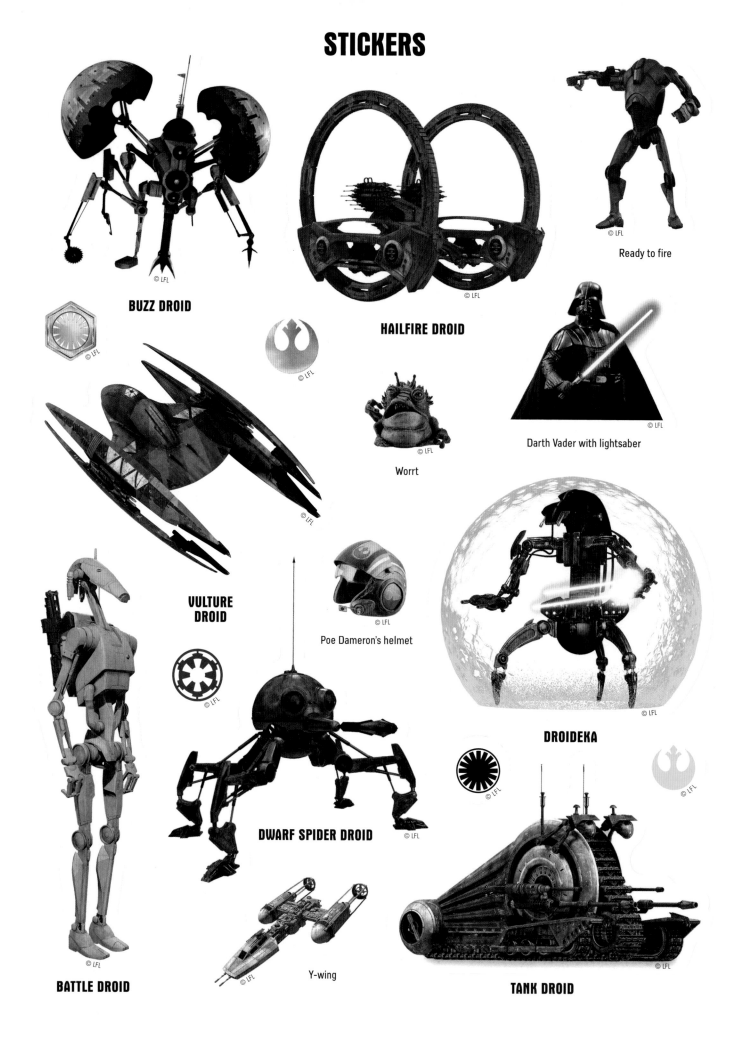

BUZZ DROID

HAILFIRE DROID

Ready to fire

Worrt

Darth Vader with lightsaber

VULTURE DROID

Poe Dameron's helmet

DROIDEKA

DWARF SPIDER DROID

Y-wing

BATTLE DROID

TANK DROID

STICKERS

NABOO YACHT

SNOWSPEEDER

REY'S SPEEDER

LANDSPEEDER

SKI SPEEDER

SAIL BARGE

Planet Coruscant

MILLENNIUM FALCON

Han Solo

Leia Organa

Loyal C-3PO

STICKERS

Determined Finn

TIE FIGHTER

SLAVE I

Brave Rose

U-WING

RESISTANCE BOMBER

A-WING

DAGOBAH

Maz Kanata

JEDI INTERCEPTOR

HOTH

STICKERS

TATOOINE

NABOO

ENDOR

AHCH-TO

CORUSCANT

Captain Phasma's helmet

Anakin's podracer

CANTONICA

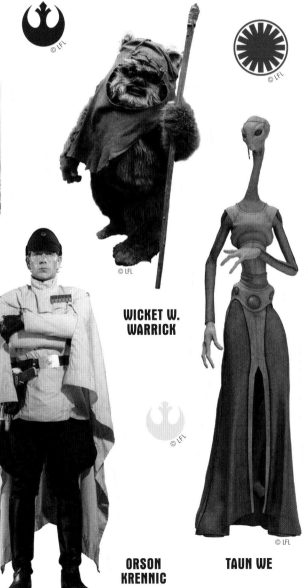

WICKET W. WARRICK

ORSON KRENNIC

TAUN WE

STICKERS

Rey's lightsaber

UNKAR PLUTT

NIEN NUNB

CARETAKER

JAR JAR BINKS

HAPPABORE

JABBA THE HUTT

FATHIER

VARACTYL

STICKERS

Helpful B-U4D

BANTHA

TAUNTAUN

DEWBACK

WAMPA

SPACE SLUG

VULPTEX

NEXU

ACKLAY

STICKERS

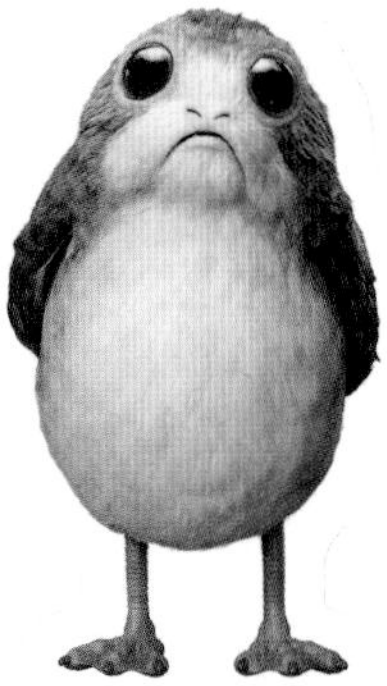

Cute porg

SARLACC

RANCOR

OPEE SEA KILLER

BOBA FETT

Praetorian helmet

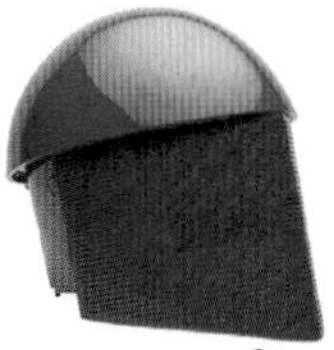

GREEDO

JANGO FETT

DJ

BOSSK

IG-88

X-wing pilot helmet

STICKERS

Flapping porg

LANDO CALRISSIAN

Chewbacca

L3-37

Han Solo

K-2SO running

Poe in flight gear

THERM SCISSORPUNCH

Kylo Ren

SIDON ITHANO

DRYDEN VOS

EXTRA STICKERS

EXTRA STICKERS

EXTRA STICKERS

EXTRA STICKERS

EXTRA STICKERS

EXTRA STICKERS